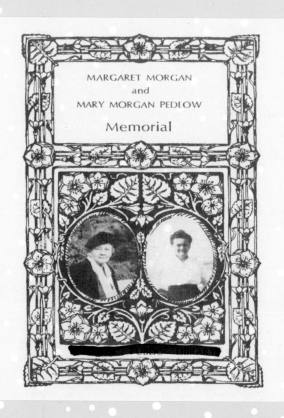

MARGARET MORGAN
and
MARY MORGAN PEDLOW

Memorial

MOVE-ALONG

NURSERY RHYMES

Rookie
Nursery
Rhymes™

Children's Press®
An Imprint of Scholastic Inc.

Library of Congress Cataloging-in-Publication Data

Names: Huliska-Beith, Laura, 1964- illustrator. | Hefferan, Rob, illustrator.
| Allyn, Virginia, illustrator.
Title: Move-along nursery rhymes.
Description: New York, NY : Children's Press, an imprint of Scholastic Inc.,
[2016] | ?2017 | Series: Rookie nursery rhymes | Summary: Includes three
traditional nursery rhyme, illustrated by different artists.
Identifiers: LCCN 2016007878| ISBN 9780531228784 (library binding) | ISBN
9780531229644 (pbk.)
Subjects: LCSH: Nursery rhymes. | Children's poetry. | CYAC: Nursery rhymes.
Classification: LCC PZ8.3 .M8627 2016 | DDC 398.8—dc23 LC record available at http://lccn.loc.gov/2016007878

Produced by Spooky Cheetah Press
Design by Book & Look

Printed in China 62

1 2 3 4 5 6 7 8 9 10 R 25 24 23 22 21 20 19 18 17 16

Illustrations by Laura Huliska-Beith (Jack and Jill), Rob Heffernan (Little Boy Blue),
Virginia Allyn (Little Miss Muffet), and pp 6–12, 14–20, 22–28 (wooden bar) Venimo/Shutterstock

TABLE OF CONTENTS

JACK
AND JILL

Illustrated by Laura Huliska-Beith

Listen to the
audio here:

http://www.scholastic.com/NR10

Jack and Jill

went up the hill

to fetch

a pail of water.

Jack fell down

and broke his crown,

and Jill came tumbling after.

LITTLE BOY BLUE

Illustrated by Rob Heffernan

Little Boy Blue,
come blow your horn.

The sheep's in the meadow.

The cow's in the corn.

Where is the boy who
looks after the sheep?

He's in the haystack
fast asleep.

Will you wake him?
No, not I!

For if I do,
he's sure to cry.

LITTLE
MISS MUFFET

Illustrated by Virginia Allyn

Little Miss Muffet

sat on a tuffet,

eating some curds and whey.

Along came a spider,

who sat down beside her,

and frightened

Miss Muffet away!

FUN WITH

NURSERY RHYMES

FUN WITH

Jack and Jill

Pages 5 to 12

Jack and Jill are outdoors. There are many flowers in the grass. There is also a butterfly that follows them up and down the hill.

Go back and count:

- How many red flowers can you find?

- How many times does the beautiful butterfly appear?

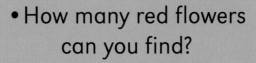

FUN WITH

Little Boy Blue
Pages 13 to 20

Little Boy Blue works on a farm looking after sheep. There are many other animals on his farm, too.

Take another look through the book.

- How many sheep can you count?
- What sound does the sheep make?
- How many cows can you count?
- What sound does the cow make?

Little Miss Muffet
Pages 21 to 28

Wow, Miss Muffet is really afraid of that spider! She was so scared that she ran away.

Move like the characters in the story:

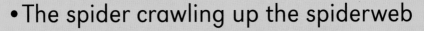

- The spider crawling up the spiderweb
- Little Miss Muffet eating curds and whey
- Little Miss Muffet running away